For Gordon Littlejohn – S.P.
For Mark and Sean, "brothers and friends" – R.J.

Text copyright © 2007 Simon Puttock
Illustrations copyright © 2007 Russell Julian
Original edition published in England by Oxford University Press 2007

Printed in Singapore

Library of Congress Cataloging-in-Publication Data

Puttock, Simon.
Goat and Donkey in the Great Outdoors / Simon Puttock ; illustrated by Russell Julian.
p. cm.
Summary: Goat decides to take a vacation to the Great Outdoors, but eventually ends up right where he started.
ISBN-13: 978-1-56148-573-4 (hardcover)
[1. Vacations–Fiction. 2. Goats–Fiction. 3. Donkeys–Fiction.
4. Friendship–Fiction.]   I. Julian, Russell, 1975-   , ill. II. Title.
PZ7.P9835Go 2007
[E]–dc22
2006027204

Simon Puttock and Russell Julian

Goat and Donkey
in The Great Outdoors

Good Books

Intercourse, PA 17534
800/762-7171
www.GoodBooks.com

One morning, Goat announced, "I have decided to take a vacation. A vacation in the Great Outdoors!"
"What a good idea," said Donkey. "While you are away I will have peace and quiet to read my book."

"Goody," said Goat. "That's settled then."

But a little while later, Goat said, "Donkey, where do you think
I should GO on my vacation?"
"Goodness," said Donkey. "Haven't you decided yet?"
"No," said Goat. "But I want to go somewhere special."

"Well," said Donkey, "do you want a hot place or a cold place?"
"Hmm...," said Goat. "I think somewhere in between."

"Do you want to get wet, or do you want to stay dry?" asked Donkey.

"A bit of both, please," said Goat.

"And what about being high up,
or low down?" asked Donkey.
"Flat in the middle
would be grand," Goat decided.

"And do you want a quiet
vacation, or an exciting one?"

"Goodness," said Goat. "There's more
to the Great Outdoors than I realized!
I'll think about it and let you know."

At lunch Goat said, "Donkey, I have thought and thought, and I have decided that I would like to go somewhere just like here. Do you know a special somewhere that is just like here?"

Donkey laughed. "Goat," he said,
"there is only *one* special place that is
Just Like Here."

"Goody," said Goat.
"Then that is where I will go."
And he trotted off to
finish his packing.

"But Goat," said Donkey, "that special place is HERE!"
"Goody and GOODY!" said Goat.
"Then I will have my vacation RIGHT HERE!
I will put up my tent in the garden
and everything will be perfect."

Goat snuggled down in his sleeping bag.
He felt very peaceful and quiet.
Perhaps a little TOO quiet.

"Donkey!" Goat called.
"Yes, Goat?"

"Would you like to come on my
vacation with me?
It's too quiet without you."

"Can I bring my book with me?
And some games? And my very special blanket?"
"Yes," said Goat.
"In that case," said Donkey, "I would love to."
Donkey squashed into the tent and snuggled down.

"Donkey," said Goat.
"Yes, Goat?" said Donkey.

"It's STILL too quiet."
"Well," said Donkey, "we could play catch."

But it's hard to play catch in a tent.

And IMPOSSIBLE to play football.
And ping-pong in a tent is just SILLY!

"Perhaps," said Goat, "we should do something
QUITE quiet after all."
"I know," said Donkey. "How about a story?"
"I like stories," said Goat.
"Then we shall have an exciting story,
all about the Great Outdoors."
"Oh goody," said Goat, "yes, please!"

And that is exactly what they did.

THE END

THE END

THE END

Why do people
get milk
from cows,
why do some people
sell them